Weekly Reader Books

The Ghost at Penniman House

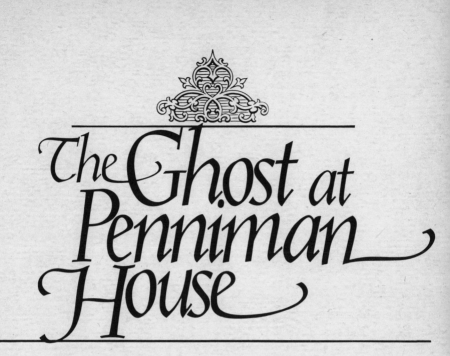

The Ghost at Penniman House

by Wilma Pitchford Hays

Illustrated
by Loretta Krupinski

Xerox Education Publications

Text copyright © 1979 by Wilma Pitchford Hays

Illustrations copyright © 1979 by Xerox Education Publications

Publishing, Executive and Editorial Offices:
Xerox Education Publications
Middletown, Connecticut 06457

Library of Congress Catalog Card Number: 78-78364

Xerox® is a trademark of Xerox Corporation.

CONTENTS

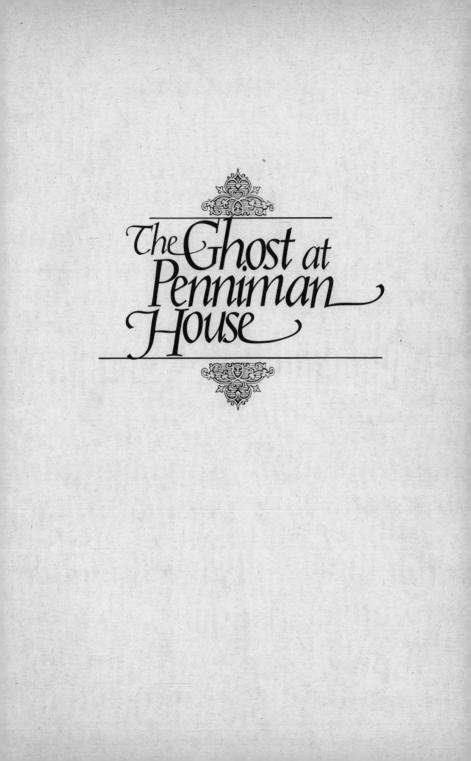

The Ghost at Penniman House

1

The Ghost of Caleb Rich

Betty Rich tossed a *Cape Cod Standard Times* onto the porch of the last house on her newspaper route. She turned her bike quickly and rode fast along Fort Hill Road through a tunnel of trees. She wanted to get back past the deserted Penniman House before the sun set completely.

Aunt Hattie had said that the ghost of Caleb Rich had returned to the house. Betty had never seen a ghost. She didn't want to meet one for the first time after dark.

"You'll know Caleb," Aunt Hattie had said. "He has a tangle of dark hair, and he always has that black hound with him."

Betty raced around a curve and up an incline. Even at dusk the large yellow Victorian Penniman House was beautiful. She and her cousin, Steve, had played here before the Cape Cod National Seashore Park had bought the house and boarded up the windows. Tonight it looked lonely among the tall trees and brush and creeper vines.

Captain Penniman had built the house more than a hundred years ago. He had brought back, from his whaling hunts, the jawbones of a giant whale and set them up for a gateway.

Betty glanced at the bleached white jawbones and saw a young man standing between them. He looked exactly as Aunt Hattie had described Caleb. He had dark curly hair, and his hand was on the head of a lean hound beside him. This hound was tan, but maybe ghost hounds didn't keep their color.

Betty's heart beat faster. She rose in her bike seat, leaned forward, and pedaled furiously along the narrow road until she reached the Cape Highway. It was dark when she finally came to her home.

Her cousin, Steve Winslow, had returned from his newspaper route and was waiting for her in the driveway between their two houses.

"What's wrong?" he asked. "Did you see the ghost? You look pale enough to be one!"

She was too scared to get mad at his teasing smile, but she had to get her breath before she could answer. She just looked at him.

Steve and Betty didn't look like cousins, although his mother and her father were sister and brother. Steve was blonde, his hair almost white from a summer of sunning on the beach and pitching Little League baseball. Her hair was as curly and black as the young man's she had seen in the whalebone gateway. She was six weeks older than Steve, but he had sprouted up half a head taller. He was slender as a willow tree, while Betty was round enough to hope that she'd take off a few pounds riding her bike on the paper route.

"Aunt Hattie is right," she said at last. "The ghost of Caleb Rich is back at the Penniman House. Caleb and his hound, too."

Steve looked at her as if he thought she was playing a trick. "Betty," he said, "you're as cuckoo as Aunt Hattie."

"You know she's not cuckoo," Betty said. "She's just very old and sometimes a little absent-minded."

"Absent-minded, addle-pated, off-her-rocker, anything you want to call it," Steve said as he walked to the garage with Betty to put her bicycle away. "But she sure remembers anything that happened a hundred years ago." He flipped the electric switch and flooded the garage with light.

"Aunt Hattie's only ninety-seven," Betty said. "She was born when the Penniman House was almost new. She remembers that her older brother, Caleb, sailed as a whaleman with Captain Penniman. Then, when there were no more whales to be caught, Caleb worked for Captain Penniman here. She remembers the terrible night when Caleb was killed by lightning in the Penniman orchard."

Steve nodded. He had heard her tell about the storm.

"Aunt Hattie says that Caleb has come back only three times—and each time when something was wrong at the Penniman place," Betty said. "What's wrong there now, Steve?"

He stood with his hand on the light switch and looked at Betty. His teasing smile was gone. "Are you going to tell Aunt Hattie what you think you saw?" he asked.

"What I *saw,*" Betty corrected him.

"Someone could have been looking at the house and stood in the gateway," Steve argued. "We've stood there. Tourists take pictures of one another between the gateway lots of times."

"It was too dark to take pictures," Betty answered. "November's not tourist season. No one goes down that road at night except the family beyond the last place where I deliver the paper, and I know all of them."

Steve didn't have an answer. He turned off the light and walked with Betty to the kitchen door. He knew his cousin almost as well as he knew himself. They had lived all their lives in houses built side by side on Grandpa Rich's land. Betty wasn't the kind of girl to see things that weren't there. Until tonight he hadn't thought she would believe in ghosts either. But she lived in Great-aunt Hattie Rich's house, and the old lady had some strange ideas.

As Betty opened the door Steve said, "It was almost dark when you passed the Penniman House. One of the tall trees could have cast a shadow the height of a man. And anyone's hound could be out for a run."

"Trees don't have a head of dark curly hair," Betty said, "and I never saw this hound before. Aunt Hattie told me three days ago that Caleb was back. I don't know how she knew. I've got to tell her that I saw him there." ☐

2
Great-aunt Hattie's Scrimshaw

Betty came into the kitchen. Her mother, making an apple salad, smiled and said, "I'm glad you're home. It gets dark so early now."

Betty tossed her jacket on a chair and sniffed. "Something smells good. Is supper ready?"

"Almost," her mother said, "but your father's not home yet. Please take Aunt Hattie's supper up to her."

Betty took a plate and filled it with pot roast, mashed potatoes, and green beans. Aunt Hattie had a good appetite and wanted her supper before the rest of the family was ready to eat. She was too frail to come down the stairs alone, so she often had supper in her room.

Betty climbed the stairs carrying a tray of food. The door to Aunt Hattie's room was open. Betty put the tray on a table and switched on the light. The old lady was asleep in her chair and did not wake. Before her on a low table was spread her collection of scrimshaw.

Many times Betty had seen the beautiful carvings made from the jawbones and teeth of whales. The old lady never got tired of looking at them and telling the story of each piece.

Betty looked again at the eighteen ''jagging wheels,'' each a delicate white figure carved with a scalloped bone wheel at one end. The wheel was used to crimp pastry around the edge of a pie.

Aunt Hattie woke suddenly and sat up. She opened her eyes and looked around as if she wondered where she was.

''I brought your supper,'' Betty said. ''I'll bring up your tea as soon as I make it.''

Aunt Hattie was always cheered by food. She patted Betty's hand. ''You're a good child,'' she said.

Betty picked up the jagging wheels and placed them carefully in the fitted compartments of the blue velvet-lined box in which Aunt Hattie stored them. There were a small flying fish, a horse, a serpent, a sword, a windmill, and several kinds of flower blooms. But the carving that Betty liked best was a little hound dog with the pastry crimping wheel between his front paws.

Aunt Hattie saw her holding the hound and smiled. ''Caleb carved that,'' she said. ''It was his own hound, you know. It went everywhere with him. It was killed when he was.''

Betty placed the dog in the box and turned to her great-aunt. ''Aunt Hattie,'' she said, ''you were right. I saw Caleb tonight standing in the jawbones of the whale in the gateway. His hound was with him.''

Aunt Hattie went on eating her supper, unconcerned. Betty wondered if she had heard her.

Finally Aunt Hattie said, with her mouth almost too full,

"Did you tell him I'm expecting him to come see me?"

"I was too scared," Betty said. "I rode my bike as fast as I could to get home."

Aunt Hattie looked surprised. "Caleb wouldn't hurt a fly," she said, "and that hound dog of his wouldn't either. Unless he thought someone was trying to hurt Caleb. Then he'd attack. He loved that boy."

"Boy?" Betty asked. "I thought he was twenty when he died."

"He was," Aunt Hattie said. "But he was only fifteen when he went to sea with Captain Penniman. I always think of him the age he was when I waved goodbye to him. I was seven then."

Betty went to the kitchen and made tea and took it up to Aunt Hattie. She heard her father's car come into the driveway.

"I'll be back up," she told Aunt Hattie. "Mama's got supper on because Papa has to keep the gas station open until nine tonight."

As they were eating, her father said, "Your mother's going back to town with me. She's on the committee to decorate the church for harvest supper. Think you can hold down the fort until nine?"

Betty gave him an "of-course-I-can" look. She had stayed several nights when her parents were both busy. They never left Aunt Hattie to get to bed alone.

"I'll ask Steve over to do homework with me," she said.

"He has Sea Scouts tonight," her mother said. "We're to pick him up and bring him home when we come."

Betty didn't want to say that she wasn't too happy about staying alone tonight. It wasn't as easy to speak to her father and mother about a ghost as it was to Aunt Hattie. They were eating dessert before she was able to tell them what she had seen. "I was passing the Penniman House tonight," she said. "I saw Caleb Rich standing in the jawbone gateway."

"Caleb Rich?" her mother asked, as if she couldn't think who he could be.

Her father knew. He had grown up with Aunt Hattie. "She means the family ghost," he said. "He hasn't been back in forty years."

"Ghost?" her mother asked. "Back?"

Her father answered, but he looked at Betty. "Caleb was Aunt Hattie's older brother," he said. "Betty, you must remember that Aunt Hattie is very old. Sometimes she gets today mixed with things that happened eighty years ago. You mustn't believe everything you hear. You know there are no ghosts."

"I *saw* him," Betty said.

"You saw someone," her father said firmly. "You didn't see Caleb Rich. He's been dead eighty years or more. Now don't forget to keep the doors locked while we're away."

"The telephone numbers of the gas station and the church are right on the refrigerator door," her mother added. "We'll be back a few minutes after nine."

"Yes," Betty said. They always told her to keep the doors locked and where the telephone numbers were, although they had been in the same place for years. It was no use trying to talk to them about ghosts, either. They were both sure there were no ghosts, and that was that.

When they had gone, she put the dishes in the dishwasher, all except the knives. She washed and dried those by hand. Her mother said dishwasher heat could loosen the cement in the handles of the old silver that had belonged to Aunt Hattie.

At eight o'clock she went up to see if her great-aunt was ready for bed. Betty brought a fresh glass of water from the bathroom and placed it on the night table. The old lady opened her eyes.

"Will you put my scrimshaw away?" she asked. "I forgot to do it."

Betty picked up the worn blue box. "When our class visited the museum in New Bedford," she said, "the director told us that really good old scrimshaw is valuable now."

"Aye," Aunt Hattie said. "No one takes the time to carve like that any more. On the whaling ships, the men had to wait and wait and wait for the sight of whales. They were at sea for two and three years at a time. Between whale sightings, they had little to do. Caleb said he'd go crazy if he didn't carve."

Betty was about to place the blue box in the top drawer of the dresser where Aunt Hattie kept it. She hesitated. "I guess this old scrimshaw is worth thousands of dollars now," she said. "Do you think it should be kept where it's so easy to find? For a thief to find, I mean?"

Aunt Hattie frowned. "I thought of that this summer," she said, "when there were so many break-ins around here. But the thieves seemed to take only old silver and expensive jewels."

Betty opened the top drawer. "Thieves probably don't know what old scrimshaw is worth," she said. "Besides, there hasn't been a burglary since summer."

"Still," Aunt Hattie said, "the police never caught the thieves. Maybe you had better put the box in Papa's old sea chest under the window. I keep the key pinned behind the draperies."

Betty found the key, unlocked the chest, and placed the blue box on top of quilts that smelled of pine and dried sweet fern. When she had closed the lid, she knelt on the chest and looked out of the window toward the Penniman House.

Though the moon was high, she couldn't see the old house because of the many trees around it. Then she thought of something.

"Aunt Hattie," she said. "You asked me to tell Caleb you wanted to see him. If you haven't seen him, how did you know he was there?"

"Oh, I heard his hound overhead in full cry," Aunt Hattie said. "They passed over the house but didn't stop. I knew where they were going."

Betty turned and stared at Aunt Hattie, almost as frightened as she had been when she saw the young man in the gateway. But the old lady looked perfectly natural. She always spoke in a soft voice and she didn't raise it now. She pulled herself up in bed and leaned on an elbow.

"Listen," she said. "You can hear Caleb's hound now. A long way off, but I'd know his cry anywhere."

Betty could hear something. She looked through the window. There against the moon was a V formation of wild geese, a dozen or more, high in the sky. She could hear their faint, lonely cry. It wasn't honking. From far away the wild geese did sound like the hunting cry of a hound who had sighted a fox.

Betty went to the bed and pulled the blanket up over her aunt, who lay back again on her pillow.

"It sounds like a hound," Betty said, "but I saw them, Aunt Hattie. We heard the cry of wild geese."

Aunt Hattie did not look convinced.

Betty turned out the light. Only the night bulb in the bathroom and the moon shining through the window illuminated the room. "Goodnight, Aunt Hattie," she said.

"Goodnight," Aunt Hattie answered. "You don't need to be afraid of Caleb or his hound, Betty. When you meet, he'll know you're one of the family. You look like him." □

3
Nauset Marsh

A----

All week Betty saw nothing unusual as she passed the Penniman House to deliver the newspaper. In one way, she was relieved. On the other hand, she was a little disappointed. Aunt Hattie had almost convinced her that the ghost of Caleb Rich would not hurt her. If this were true, it would be exciting to meet him—in daylight.

Then, on Saturday afternoon, Betty and Steve rode their bikes along Fort Hill Road. Cameras bobbed in carrying-cases over their shoulders. They planned to take pictures along the Fort Hill Nature Trail set up by the Cape Cod National Seashore Park.

Their teacher had asked the girls and boys in the fifth grade to write a story about some area near them and illustrate it with snapshots they had taken themselves. The best papers would be shown at the parent-teacher meeting after Thanksgiving.

"I'm going to write about whaling in the old days," Steve said. "Dad says Captain Penniman was a very successful whaler. His house and the whalebone gateway are special. I want pictures of them."

Betty glanced at the gateway, remembering the young man who had stood there at dusk beside his hound. Steve saw her and grinned.

"Too bad I can't get a picture of your ghost," he teased.

"You can get pictures on the way back," Betty said. "The light is just right now on Nauset Marsh, and that's what I'm writing about."

They left their bikes at the Fort Hill parking lot and ran along the trail. Betty stopped to look at a lone orange and black monarch butterfly fanning its wings above the silvery floss of an open milkweed pod.

"You're here pretty late," she said to it. "All your friends have flown south." She snapped a picture of the monarch.

She didn't try to catch up with Steve, who had gone way ahead of her. She liked being all alone to hear the twitter and flutter of birds in the grasses and brush that were higher than her head. She walked softly along the trail and heard the call of a chickadee. A moment later she saw its black-capped head. Then a dozen goldfinch rose from feeding on the wild thistle seed they loved. They flew a short distance and watched until she went by them toward the large boulder left on this land in glacial times.

From the boulder she looked out on Nauset Marsh, salt water winding through islands of coarse grass. Her father had told her that many marine animals were born and grew up in these salt marshes.

She climbed onto the boulder and took a picture of the

marsh. It was too bad a snapshot couldn't show what a great food plant the marsh was. It fed tiny lobsters, clams, flounder, striped bass and wild fowl.

Beyond the marsh, she could see the Atlantic Ocean, whose waters tumbled on and on until they reached Spain. She listened to the sound of the sea. It was not the booming roar of storm surf that she sometimes heard grinding at the shore and dragging away sand and rocks. Today there was a quieter sound of water that is never still, breakers rolling up onto beach stones, then running downhill again into the sea. Betty knew this sound was always there, but she was hardly ever alone and quiet enough to hear it.

"Got-chu," Steve yelled as he jumped from behind and caught her ankle.

Betty squealed and almost fell off the boulder. She grabbed his blonde hair and pulled.

"Ouch," he called. "I give up."

"You're mean," she said, and jumped to the ground.

Quickly he tried to distract her. "What do you think that big spike's driven into the boulder for?" he asked. "Think the Indians tied up their enemies here? Or maybe the Pilgrims tied up the kids that whispered in church."

"You ought to be tied to it," she said in disgust. But she couldn't stay angry with him long. He was a good companion, interested in almost everything she was.

"Papa says the spike has probably been in this boulder more than two hundred years," she said. "Probably used to

pull barges of salt marsh hay ashore. That's what the early settlers here fed to their livestock.''

Steve glanced at the sun. ''We'd better hurry,'' he said, ''or I won't have light enough to take pictures at the Penniman place.''

Betty ran ahead of him along the trail. She reached her bike first and bent to pick it up. She screamed, turned, and ran straight into Steve. He caught her arm and cried, ''What's the matter?''

She could only gasp in terror.

''Did you see the ghost?'' he asked.

She shook her head.

Steve looked exasperated, but worried. ''Then what?''

''A toad,'' she whispered. ''I almost touched a toad.''

Steve kept hold of her arm and said gently, ''I'll bring your bike to you, Betty.''

She was still trembling when he came, wheeling her bike. ''Thank you,'' she said.

He rode beside her, saying nothing. Steve understood her phobia about toads. All her life, to see a toad was like a nightmare to her. She knew toads wouldn't hurt her. She knew, but she couldn't do anything about her terror. Steve teased her about everything else, but never about her unreasonable fear. He tried to comfort her now.

''I think you saw a piece of dried mud dropped off the wheel of someone's car,'' he said. ''That's all I saw when I got your bike.''

She was still shivery and not over her fright when they stopped before the Penniman House.

"I don't think you'll come upon a toad this late in the fall," Steve said, "but you can wait here in the road. It won't take me long to go around back and take a snapshot of the carriage house, or whatever Captain Penniman called that building at the back end of the house."

"I'll go with you," Betty said. ☐

4
The Ring

Betty followed Steve along the overgrown path close to the west wall of the yellow house. "Careful of the poison ivy," he warned.

"The creepers are worse," Betty said, as she caught an ankle in one of the strong ropelike vines that twisted along the ground everywhere. By the time she had untangled herself, Steve had turned a corner at the back. She caught up with him at the open end of the carriage house.

"Maybe Captain Penniman built this for a stable," she said, peering into the dark interior. "There're stalls for horses."

"And plenty of room for a carriage or two," he said, winding his camera. "A nice dark place for a ghost to hang out."

He was grinning. Betty stepped inside the wide doorway to get out of the chill wind that had begun to blow from the sea. It was quiet as a cave in here.

She stood and listened. She heard a soft sound as if someone was humming. Where was it coming from, in this deserted place?

"Steve," she whispered, "are you humming?"

He stepped inside the doorway. "No," he said.

"Listen," she whispered.

She knew by the expression on his face that he heard it too, now. "It can't be anyone in the house," he said. "The windows are boarded over to keep people out until the house is restored."

Together they stood in the doorway. The sound seemed to come from somewhere among the trees. "From the direction of the orchard," Betty said, "where Caleb was killed."

They peered around the doorpost. They could see nothing but brush and creepers under tall trees. The humming turned to singing, a man's voice so soft they could barely hear the words.

> My lay was one in two hundred,
> Only one in two hundred,
> Yet he cheated me of that.
> Aye, he cheated me of that.

"An old whaling chanty," Betty whispered. "Aunt Hattie has sung it to me. Steve, do you think Caleb is out there?"

"No," he said, "but it's someone who knows old folk songs. What's he singing about, Betty?"

"The share each whaleman was paid," she said, "his share of the profits on the whales taken on a trip at sea."

The singing stopped, followed by a new sound, the muffled chip-chip of a spade striking into hard earth. Betty put her hand on Steve's arm.

"It *is* Caleb. Aunt Hattie said he was planting a tree here when the storm came up and he was killed.''

Steve shook his head, but he looked troubled. ''No one comes here this time of year,'' he said, ''especially near dark.''

''That's what he thinks, too, or he'd be more quiet,'' Betty said. ''What is he digging for?''

''I'm going to find out,'' Steve said. ''Wait here.'' He disappeared around the corner of the building before she could follow.

She waited, her heart beating loudly again. She couldn't hear the sound of the spade anymore. Had the man heard Steve? She wished she knew where her cousin was. She wished he'd come back.

She heard footsteps coming and ran to meet Steve. ''Did you see him?'' she asked. ''What was he digging?''

In the dusk someone stopped suddenly before her. She could see only the dark outline of a figure taller than Steve, with a tangle of dark hair. The man was carrying a bag. It looked like a paper bag of groceries.

Caleb? Could it be Caleb? She shrank back into the shadows.

He turned and ran. She heard him cry out as he tripped over a creeping vine across the path. He fell hard, then was up and running again.

Steve raced around the corner of the house and stopped beside Betty. They listened to the man crashing through the brush.

"He was no ghost," Steve said. "I don't know what was buried here. Whatever it was, he had finished digging and started back before I got to him."

"He wouldn't have run," Betty said, "if he had a right to be here."

"Not unless he thought *you* were a ghost," Steve said. Then, "We'd better get out of here."

Betty hurried along the path after him. She remembered the creeper and stepped high to avoid it. Her foot came down on something hard as a stone. In the dusk she almost missed seeing a small box that looked like a discarded marshmallow. She didn't think it had been there when they came in. She picked it up and ran to catch up with Steve.

They wasted no time getting on their bikes and racing home. The man could be in the bushes watching them.

Her mother was backing the car onto the highway as Betty and Steve rode into the yard. She braked and called to Betty, "I'm taking supper to your father. He has to work. I'll buy groceries before I come home."

"Okay," Betty called.

When they were safely inside the garage, Betty switched on the overhead light. She stepped into a corner where no one could see her from the road, and took the small box from her pocket. Steve bent over it with her.

"Anything in it?" he asked.

"It's a box that rings come in," Betty said. She pressed the catch and the lid flew open. It was a ring. A large white stone sparkled in the light.

"A diamond," Steve said, "the size of a pea. That's worth a lot of money if it's real."

"It must be real," Betty said. "No one would bury a fake diamond."

"Nobody would bury a ring that he didn't have to hide, either," Steve said. "It must be stolen."

"He had a large paper bag in his hand," Betty said. "I bet he dug up more than this ring."

"He fell hard," Steve agreed. "The ring could have bounced out of the larger bag. He must be a thief, Betty."

"Maybe he was the thief who stole so much jewelry from homes this summer," Betty suggested.

"He could have hidden it there until the police hunt quieted down," Steve said. "Who'd find his loot buried under brush near a deserted house?"

"Do you think he knows I found the ring?" Betty asked. "Did he see me pick it up? Will he come looking for it?"

"He was too interested in getting away," Steve said. "But he may come back to hunt for it. When he doesn't find it, he'll guess we have it."

"Right," Betty said. "As soon as Papa comes home, he'll take it to the police."

"We'd better get it to the police ourselves, right now," Steve said. "I'll take it."

Betty held onto the box, not sure.

"You go in the house," Steve said. "I'll pretend to go home, but I'll ride behind our house and back onto the road again. If the thief did follow us and is watching, he'll think I went in our back door.''

Betty closed the box and dropped it into Steve's hand. He put it in his pocket.

''It would be great if the police caught the thief at the Penniman House looking for this,'' she said.

''Act natural,'' Steve warned her. He whistled as he rode his bike toward his home.

Betty left the garage and stood a moment under the light above the kitchen door. If anyone were watching, he could see that she had nothing in her hands as she went into the house. □

5
Ghost or Thief

"**D**id you see any goldfinch today?" Aunt Hattie asked when Betty took her supper to her. "When I was a girl, the fields above Nauset Marsh were gold and black with hundreds of those little birds eating wild thistle seed."

"I saw about a dozen today," Betty said.

She didn't think she should mention the thief at Penniman House until after he had been caught. There was no use exciting an old lady.

"I was hoping you'd see Caleb," Aunt Hattie said. "Over the years lots of folks around here have seen Caleb. They've told me. Once Gabe Elderedge was bringing in his lobster pots, about dark, and he saw a man appear on top of the dunes."

Betty nodded. Aunt Hattie was going to talk tonight, and when she talked, nothing would stop her. Betty only half-listened, for she had heard her great-aunt's tales over and over.

"Gabe said the man looked like Caleb. He was carrying a bag, heavy, secretly," Aunt Hattie went on. "I don't know why Caleb was carrying a bag away over on the dunes."

"A bag?" Betty asked. She was listening now. "A grocery bag?"

"A heavy bag," Aunt Hattie said. "Then while Gabe watched, Caleb just faded away, like fog or mist."

Betty was confused. Was it possible that the man tonight at the Penniman House *was* a ghost? A ghostly Caleb carrying a bag that wasn't real?

She knew that some people said that the man who haunted the old place was Captain Penniman himself. He was said to return now and then to the house he had built with whaling money. People said they'd heard him call, as if to his crew, "There go the flukes," and "Clear the boats!," as he had in the old days at sea when he sighted a whale.

She knew it wasn't the captain who dug up the ring and appeared tonight. This was a much younger man.

"Aunt Hattie," she asked, "do you think that Caleb—or any ghost—can sing?"

"Oh, yes," Aunt Hattie said, "if he's a whaleman he can. Caleb said making up verses kept them from going crazy when they were years at sea."

Aunt Hattie began to hum and chant:

Oh, the whale is free, of the boundless sea,

He lives for a thousand years,

He sinks to his rest on the billows' breast,

Not the toughest tempest fears.

Betty frowned. She had heard that old sea song before, not too long ago, and not from Aunt Hattie. Where? Who had sung it?

Tonight a man had dug with a spade and chanted, but not this sea song. Then she knew. Last summer, each week, several young men and women had gathered on the grass under the trees down by the library. They sang folk songs and people stopped and sang with them. She and Steve had joined the group one night while her mother was in the library. Did one of those folk singers have dark curly hair? She couldn't remember.

Then she heard a whistle outside the house. Steve must be back after delivering the ring to the police.

The ring, she thought, was real. She was sure of one thing now. A man who dropped a real ring was not a ghost, no matter what Aunt Hattie thought. She ran downstairs to meet Steve.

Steve's bike was sprawled across the driveway, dropped where he stopped. He stood under the light.

"Did you give the police the ring?" Betty asked.

He nodded, breathless from pedaling hard.

"What did they say?"

"Thanked me, that's all," he said.

"No questions?" Betty said. "I don't understand."

"There's a lot I don't understand," Steve said. "The man—the thief—was at the police station before I was. As soon as I was inside, I saw this young man with dark curly hair. He was sitting opposite the police chief. The paper bag of jewelry, if it was jewelry, was on the desk between them. The thief's back was to me, so I handed the ring box to the of-

ficer at the outer desk and said quick, 'We found this.' Then I got out of there.''

''You didn't give him time to ask questions,'' Betty said.

''I was so surprised to see the man there with the stuff he had dug up at the Penniman orchard,'' Steve said. ''All I could think was that I didn't want him to know we were the kids who had seen him.''

''Did the police officer recognize you?'' Betty asked.

''He probably did,'' Steve said. ''He and Dad are friends. Maybe I shouldn't have run, but it was such a switch. I wasn't expecting the thief there ahead of me.''

Betty nodded. ''When the officer sees what you handed him, you'll have a caller,'' she said.

''I hope it's the police and not the thief,'' Steve said as he turned toward home.□

6
Truth or Lie

Betty locked the kitchen door and stood with her back against it. She didn't know what to think. Why would a thief dig up something valuable, then take it directly to the police? Maybe he knew she and Steve had seen him, and thought he might save himself by turning in the jewelry first, with some kind of story.

She heard a car come into the garage and she glanced at the clock above the sink. Ten after nine. That should be her father and mother. She heard their key turn in the lock and felt weak with relief.

She ran to her father. "I'm so glad it's you. I thought it might be the police or the thief."

He dropped the groceries on the table and turned to her. "Police?" he said. "What's going on here?"

"You're frightened," her mother said and took Betty's arm, pulling her close.

Betty told them then about stopping at the Penniman House.

"What in the world were you doing at that lonely old house after sundown?" her mother interrupted.

"Steve was going to take a few pictures for our class project," Betty explained. "Only it got dark too fast after we heard the man digging and—then I ran into him and he ran and—"

"Wait a minute," her father said. "You've lost me. Now start again, Betty."

She told all that had happened at the Penniman House, and that Steve had gone to the police station with the ring and found the thief there ahead of him.

"The man was talking to the chief of police," Betty said, "and the paper bag of jewels, we think, was on the table between them. Why would he dig the jewels up at night—secretly—then take them to the police?"

"I don't know," her father said. "I'll go down and talk to Roy." Betty knew that Roy was the policeman who often went striped bass fishing with her father.

"Don't open the door to anyone until I get back," he said.

"We'll be all right," her mother said.

She didn't say a word about its being bedtime. Betty helped her put away the groceries in cabinets and the refrigerator. Then they watched TV together until her father returned.

"What did he say?" Betty asked as soon as her father opened the door.

"Well," her father said, "Roy knew the young man. He worked at a camp here this summer and he was one of the folk singers on the green."

"I thought so," Betty said, "But Caleb could sing those songs, too, and—"

"Caleb!" her father said impatiently. "Betty, do you still believe in that ghost?"

Betty wasn't sure, so she said nothing.

Her father scarcely noticed. He had more to tell.

"His name is Ned Transford. He told the police that he *found* the bag of jewelry in the brush across from the house."

"But I heard him *digging* and singing to himself, an old whaling chanty."

"I told Roy what you told me," her father said. "He was very interested in the story. He wants to talk to you and Steve tomorrow. Could you identify the man you saw?"

"Yes," Betty said, then stopped. "Not for sure. I didn't see his face. Steve didn't either. I know how tall he was, and his hair looked curly and dark. I'd know his voice, I think."

"Roy said that without a positive identification, they will have to take his word that he found the bag of jewelry as he and his hound walked along the road. It was the dog who ran into the bushes and sniffed out the bag."

"That's what *he* said," Betty cried, "but how can we know?"

"We can't," her father said. "But he did bring back the stolen jewelry. They had no proof that he didn't find it—they had to let him go. Roy said they'd check on his past and keep a close watch on the Penniman House until they do know."

The next afternoon Betty and Steve rode side by side on

their bikes along Fort Hill Road to take pictures of the Penniman House.

"The police were very nice this morning," Betty said.
"Do you think they believed us or him?"

"They believed us all right," Steve said, "but they don't
know whether or not to believe him, too."

"You mean we could have heard another man digging?"

"I don't know," Steve said. "Ned Transford says he is
working in Providence now and comes back here weekends
because he likes the Cape. He was walking his hound and
found the bag."

"Maybe he is telling the truth," Betty said. "Maybe the
real thief dropped the bag. Or maybe the real thief knew we'd
tell, so he hid the bag in the bushes and planned to come back
for it later—but Ned found it first."

"Yeah," Steve said, "and maybe I'd better take those pictures right now. I don't want to be here past dark until after
we know where the thief is." ☐

7
The Hound

Betty and Steve waited at the crossroads of the highway for the deliveryman to drop off their afternoon newspapers. Steve was showing her the snapshots he had taken almost a week before at the Penniman place.

"I just picked these up at the camera shop," he said. "Not bad."

"You got a neat picture of the gateway," Betty said. "Papa said it was an old Cape custom to erect those great whale jawbones in front of homes. This one's about the only one left."

"I guess that's why people like to have their picture taken in it," Steve said. "Now if I'd got your ghost and his hound I'd have something really neat!"

Betty turned away. He was teasing again. *He* wasn't the one who had to pass the lonely old house every night. His delivery route was in the opposite direction.

"You haven't seen anything or heard anyone this week, have you?" Steve asked.

"Not a thing," Betty said. "Papa said the police checked out that man, Ned."

"Yeah," Steve said. "He's working in a motorcycle shop in Providence, just as he said."

"He doesn't have a police record," Betty said. "Do you think he really found that bag in the bushes?"

"If he did, then the real thief could still be around," Steve said.

"I wish that delivery van would hurry and bring our papers," Betty said, looking down the road.

"He is late delivering tonight," Steve said, "and the air smells like rain."

They were silent a moment as Steve put the snapshots back in his jacket pocket. Betty felt a change in the air. A faint stir of wind sent dried leaves scurrying along the road.

She looked at the sky. A gray cloud, like smoke, was rising over Nauset Beach way. Higher than the treetops, it rolled inland toward them.

"Fog," she said. "That will bring night in the afternoon."

"I don't know what's keeping the delivery van," Steve said. "Maybe it's already storming down Hyannis way."

Betty saw a van coming around a curve in the road. "Here he is now," she said.

The deliveryman threw a bundle of newspapers onto the grass at Steve's feet. "It's coming up a blow," he called and drove on.

Steve cut the string around the newspapers and took half of them. Betty lifted the remaining papers into the large basket on her bicycle. "Maybe we should wrap them," she said.

"We'll make it before the rain if we hurry," Steve said.

Betty rode as fast as she could toward Fort Hill Road. Few cars came this way in winter, but she met one and drew as close as she could to the edge of the narrow pavement. Then she saw the welcome blue light blinking on top of the police patrol car.

The police were keeping an eye on the Penniman House as they said they would. Still, the patrol car probably wouldn't return again for several hours.

The fog had dropped down, touching the treetops and hiding the roof of the old house. It was veiled and cut in half. The lower boarded-up windows seemed like slats nailed over the sides of a cage.

She glanced at the gateway. The tall jawbones stood out white against the deep black of the trees. Empty. Nothing there.

Her heart beat faster as she raced on to the last house on the road. She tossed the newspaper on the porch and started back.

The voice of the sea could always be heard here. Ordinarily she scarcely noticed it, but now she could hear huge breakers charging over the beach and smashing against the dune barrier. That roar meant a storm over the water. She hoped it wouldn't hit inland until she reached home.

She pedaled fast past the black void at the side of the road. This was the parking lot for the many people who wanted to walk around the Penniman House in summer. No one would be here tonight. The road she knew so well seemed wild, black, and hostile now.

Then the small headlight on her bicycle reflected light from the eyes of some creature in the road ahead of her. Two eyes almost on a level with hers. A doe? she thought. No, the shining eyes were too low. A fawn?

She drew nearer and saw a long narrow head, ears cocked high. It made a sudden whine.

A hound. A tan hound. It had to be the one she had seen between the whale jawbones with the young man with curly black hair.

Was it real or Caleb's hound? A ghost dog?

Its ears flattened and its tail stirred. Betty swerved to avoid hitting it. It raced after her, making no sound. She couldn't take a chance that it was only being playful. She leaned forward on her bicycle and pedaled as she had never done before.

The front wheel struck something in the road. The sudden jolt sent her bicycle out of control. She tried to right it, but it headed into the woods and struck a tree. She went sprawling and lost consciousness for a moment.

She opened her eyes and stared up into the dark muzzle of the hound. There was a horrible pause. She couldn't even scream. And who would hear her in this deserted place?

The hound whined, a begging whine. She felt the warm lap of its tongue on her cheek. It was comforting her. Relief made her weak.

"Good dog," she said.

It barked in delight and licked her face again.

She put an arm around its neck and pulled herself up. Her right ankle hurt when she tried to walk, but she could hobble along. The hound was so tall that she didn't have to stoop to use it as a crutch. It pulled her along, whining softly as they walked. It was taking her toward the jawbone gate. She stopped.

It barked, encouraging her.

"I don't want to go there," she said. She turned back to find her bicycle.

The headlight still shone where it lay in the tall brush. She pulled it onto the side of the road, but its chain was broken. Even if she could see, she wasn't good at fixing bikes. Steve kept their bikes in repair. He didn't mind split fingernails or grease under them. She couldn't walk all the way home with a sprained ankle. What to do?

Lightning flashed, followed at once by thunder. Blobs of icy rain struck her face. The storm was here. She had to find shelter.

Again the hound barked and whined, begging. She put her hand on his neck. He began to lead her toward the shelter of the Penniman carriage house.

She followed him as fast as she could over the creeper vines. The rain beat down as if the sky had opened and dropped a waterfall. The night was so black she could not have found her way alone. The dog led her directly through the wide-open door of the carriage house.

Here the rain beat a wild tattoo on the roof, but it was dry inside. Betty stood beside the hound, soaked and shivering. Flashes of lightning gave her brief glimpses of swaying wind-tossed trees. Her teeth chattered and she hugged her arms across her chest.

"Here, put this blanket around you," a man's voice said behind her.

She swung around but saw nothing in the darkness. Her heart was beating faster than the rain on the roof. She could scarcely breathe she was so terrified. Lightning flashed again and she saw him. A young man with curly black hair.

Was he Caleb, or a real man? ☐

8
Rescued

"Don't be afraid," the man said. He handed her a blanket, not getting too close as if he knew how frightened she was.

"Caleb?" she asked after a moment.

"Caleb?" he answered, puzzled.

She drew the blanket closer. He wasn't the ghost of Caleb or he'd know his name. Then who was hiding here? Fright and nervousness made her talk too much and too fast.

"Caleb's our family ghost," she said. "My great-aunt Hattie's brother. She says he comes here—and she thinks he's here now. She wants to see him. I thought you might be—but who are you?"

"I'm not your ghost, Caleb," he said.

Then she recognized his voice. "You're the man with the bag of jewelry. You're Ned Transford."

He didn't deny it. He said nothing. She couldn't see his face. Was he angry that she recognized him? Was he afraid that she'd tell on him now?

"What are you doing here again?" she asked. "Didn't you dig up everything last week?"

She stopped. She shouldn't have said that. Now he knew that she had heard him digging. Now he knew that she didn't believe he had found the bag as he said he had.

"I still had something to do here," he said.

"The ring you dropped," she said. "You came back to hunt for it?"

He was quiet so long that she was more troubled. If only the lightning would come again and show her his face. She drew back against the rough boards of the wall.

"You found a ring?" he asked at last.

"We took it to the police," she said. "Didn't they tell you?"

"No, nothing," he said.

"They must have known you weren't telling the truth when you said you found the bag," she said. "Why did you lie?"

A streak of lightning revealed him sitting on the side of his overturned motorcycle. His head was down, his arm over the neck of the hound. He looked up and blinked when the flash dazzled his eyes.

"I tried to protect my brother," he said. "I wanted to bring in that last piece of jewelry. I didn't know what it was but I heard something fall from the bag when I ran and stumbled."

"Were you digging—or was it your brother?" she asked.

"Me," he said. "I knew where my brother hid the stolen jewels this summer. I thought if I turned them in, the police might stop looking for the one who took them."

"How did you know—did you help him steal them?" She was interested and curious. He didn't seem like a thief.

"No," he said quickly. "My brother's in a detention home for juveniles now. He's almost sixteen. I told him if he

got into any more trouble, he'd end up in prison. He confessed to me then—what he had stolen here this summer and where the jewels were buried.''

He sounded so sad that Betty couldn't help feeling sorry for him.

''If you explain to the police,'' she said, ''maybe they'll be lenient.''

''I know it was a mistake,'' he said. ''I'm ready to tell them the truth now. But I've looked after my brother since our folks died. I just hoped I could keep him from being arrested.''

Betty didn't know what to say. The rain wasn't pounding so hard on the roof now. She went and stood again in the doorway and listened to the thunder going farther and farther away.

''The storm's almost past,'' he said. ''I'll take you home on my motorcycle.''

He rolled the motorcycle to the road, its headlight showing the way. She followed with her hand on the hound's neck.

The motorcycle started with a roar. Ned reached over and helped her climb on behind him.

''Pull your blanket up away from the wheels,'' he said.

She wrapped herself closely but still shivered from the cold.

''Hang on tight,'' he shouted, as they whizzed down Fort Hill Road.

The long-legged hound raced silently beside them.☐

9
Aunt Hattie's Visitor

The roar of the motorcycle braking in the driveway brought her mother to the kitchen door. The worried look left her face when she saw Betty.

"Your father and Steve just went to look for you," her mother called.

"We met them," Betty said. "They're turning around."

"Yes, here they are now," her mother said.

Steve was first out of the car. "What happened?" he asked Betty.

"I lost control of the bike and fell," she said.

"What scared you? A toad or a ghost?" he asked.

"The hound," she said.

Steve saw the hound then. He loved dogs and caught hold of its lean neck. "You're tired," he said to it. "Come lie by the fire and get dry." He took the dog into the house.

Betty heard her mother say to Ned, "Thank you for bringing Betty home. You must come in and dry your clothes. What a storm!"

He said, "I'm not very wet, but she's soaked." He nodded toward Betty.

Her mother said, "Betty, get into dry clothes before you take cold."

Her father said, "Come in. We appreciate your rescuing her."

They all entered the kitchen. As Betty went to her bedroom, she passed the hound stretched out before the flames in the living room fireplace. Steve knelt beside it stroking its head.

She pulled off her wet clothing and got into jeans and a warm sweater. From the kitchen she heard her mother's voice saying to Ned, "You must have supper with us. It's all ready."

"No, thank you," he said. "I'm staying with friends over on the bay shore. They'll expect me for supper."

"A cup of coffee, then," her mother said.

Ned was drinking the coffee when Betty returned to the kitchen.

"You're limping," her father said. "Did you get hurt?"

"My bicycle hit a tree and I fell," she said. "The chain's broken."

Steve called, "I'll get it and fix it tomorrow."

"Let's see your ankle," her father said.

She stood with one foot on a kitchen chair. Her father felt the ankle.

"It isn't swollen," he said. "Only scratched. Better use one of the large Band-aids after your bath tonight."

Betty was surprised by a call from the top of the stairway. "Caleb? Is that you, Caleb?"

Everyone turned and looked up. Somehow Aunt Hattie had come down the top three steps of the stairs and was leaning over the banister. She was so frail that everyone below was afraid to move for fear she would be startled and fall.

"Caleb," she said, "I knew it was you, even before I saw your hound. You've come to see me." The flames from the fireplace below lighted her face, so full of joy.

"She thinks you're her brother Caleb," Betty said to Ned in a low voice. "I told you about him."

He nodded. "The ghost," he said softly.

Her father explained quietly, "She's ninety-seven, and gets today and yesterday a little mixed up at times."

"Aunt Hattie, don't move," he called. "I'll take you back upstairs."

"No," she said. "I want Caleb."

She was looking only at Ned now. "I've been admiring that scrimshaw you carved," she said to him. "You'll want to see it again."

Ned didn't hesitate. "I'll go up," he said.

He didn't hurry on the stairs. He was careful not to unsettle her. He placed his arm around her waist and almost lifted her back to her room. Betty could hear Aunt Hattie's happy voice as she talked to him.

Her mother said, "That was most understanding of such a young man."

"You don't recognize him," Betty said. "He's the man who dug up the jewels at the Penniman place."

Her father and mother looked at her. Steve quit petting the hound and stared at her.

"The thief?" he whispered.

"He's not a thief," Betty said, "and he was good to me." She told them quickly how Ned had tried to protect his teen-age brother who was the real thief. "He's going to tell the police now, though," she said. "And he hopes the police will give his brother another chance, now that he has returned the jewels."

Her father's face was white. She couldn't tell what he was thinking. Steve looked envious that she had had an adventure without him. Her mother said, "Aunt Hattie will be hungry. Take her supper to her, Betty, and give that young man a chance to go back to his friends."

"I'll carry up the tray," Steve offered. Betty took the teapot and they went upstairs.

They could hear Aunt Hattie still talking. "No, Caleb, that hibiscus bloom is the only scrimshaw you didn't carve. You remember, you bought it off that old whaleman in Honolulu. He had carved it up in the Arctic, that time all the whaling vessels were lost in the ice field."

"Yes," Ned said, as if he knew what she was talking about. He didn't have to say much as long as he listened.

Betty and Steve stopped at the head of the stair. "She's having such a good time," Betty whispered. "I hate to interrupt her."

Steve frowned. "If we wait," he said, "she will tell him

the whole story again. How the whales grew scarcer and scarcer over the years, until the whaling fleet had to go into the Arctic through the Bering Strait for whales—and one September they didn't get out before the ice froze—and thirty-three whaling vessels had to be abandoned there.''

Betty smiled at him. They both knew the story by heart. The whaling fleet had been crushed like eggshells. But five small barks, with crews of great courage and skill, had gone in close to the grinding ice, again and again, until they had rescued every crewman and taken them all to Honolulu.

''We've got to rescue him,'' Steve said.

''Yes,'' Betty said. ''It was good of him to pretend to be Caleb.''

They went into Aunt Hattie's room with her supper. Ned stood up at once, but he took Aunt Hattie's hand and told her goodbye before he left the room.

Betty said to him, ''Thank you—and good luck.''

Betty wasn't surprised to see Steve follow him down the stairs, for her cousin loved a motorcycle.

She turned to Aunt Hattie who could always be distracted by good food. ''I've brought you Cape scallops,'' she said. ''and Mama made cranberry jell. Steve and I picked the cranberries along the edges of the bog where the machines can't reach.''

''I love fresh cranberry jell,'' Aunt Hattie said. ''We should have given Caleb some.'' She began to eat.

Betty said, ''Shall I put away your scrimshaw?''

Aunt Hattie nodded. "Some day the scrimshaw is to be yours, Betty," she said. "Caleb will like that."

Betty placed the little carved hound in its nest in the blue velvet box. She had always loved the hound best. Now she had even more reason to appreciate a hound.

She went over and put the box in the sea chest that smelled of pine and dried sweet fern. Then she knelt on the chest and looked out toward the Penniman House. Nearby the sky was still overcast and weepy, but over the Penniman orchard, it was clear. The black sky was full of stars as thick as snowflakes.

Papa and Steve were right, she thought. There was probably never a ghost over there. But she wasn't going to tell Aunt Hattie that.

"We had such a good visit," Aunt Hattie said, "and just in time. He's leaving tonight. He said so. I don't suppose Caleb will be back again for a long time."

Betty turned and looked at her. Aunt Hattie sighed but she still looked happy.

"No, I don't suppose he will," Betty said.☐

COLOPHON

Designed by Walter J. Haan.

The text is set in 12 point Times Roman with 4 points leading.
Chapter titles are set in 27 point Times Roman Italic.
The front matter is set in Post Mediaeval Light Italic with
Swing Caps and in Times Roman.
The decoration used in the front matter
is from a font of Stephen Ornate.

Composition by Eastern Typesetting Company.
Printed by offset lithography at Kingsport Press.
The Paper used is Baxter Text, Basis 45
from Great Northern Paper Company.

Cover printed at Xerox Education Center, Columbus, Ohio.
Perfect case-bound at Kingsport Press using Permalin, White,
Linen Finish, resin-impregnated paper.